Based on Real-Life Events
Two Short Stories

Alberto Rivera Zamora

All rights reserved. The total or partial reproduction of this work is not allowed, nor its incorporation into a computer system, or its transmission in any form or by any means (electronic, mechanical, photocopying, recording, or otherwise) without the prior written permission of the copyright holder is a violation of these rights and may constitute a crime against intellectual property

The content of this work is the responsibility of the author and does not necessarily reflect the views of the publishing house. All texts and images were provided by the author, who is solely responsible for their rights.

Publshed by Ibukku, LLC
www.ibukku.com
Cover Design: Ángel Flores Guerra Bistrain
Graphic Design: Diana Patricia González Juárez
Copyright © 2023 Alberto Rivera Zamora
ISBN Paperback: 978-1-68574-688-9
ISBN Hardcover: 978-1-68574-690-2
ISBN eBook: 978-1-68574-689-6

Index

INTRODUCTION	5
PANDEMIC	
(OR THE JOY OF SMILING)	9
LITERALLY	11
THE BEGINNING	12
THE CONTAGION	15
BUSINESS AS USUAL	17
A PROBLEM	19
GETTING WORSE	21
THE SOLUTION	23
EVERYTHING UNDER CONTROL	26
TRAGIC END	28
A CONSPIRACY	
SPECIES SUPERIORITY	29
SLEEPING IN TACAJÓ	31
A NEW SITUATION, YET ALL THE SAME	34
THE DOCK	39
KILLING COCKROACHES	45
WHAT IS THE "IAPS" DOING TO ME?	49
THEY DON'T KNOW	
WHO THEY'RE DEALING WITH	55
WE'VE ALWAYS BEEN DOMINATED	58
WE ARE JUST CATTLE!	62
GLIMPSES OF HOPE	64
GOD HAS MADE US SUPERIOR	66
"INTERSPECIES" HARMONY	68
THANK GOD, JUST A DREAM (?)	74

INTRODUCTION

The title does not need to be entirely objective, of course, since it pertains to two short stories. However, it is true that both are based on "REAL-LIFE EVENTS." This does not mean that I chronicle a story with absolute fidelity. In fact, it is a critique of novels or movies that claim this in an attempt to convince the audience that[1] what is described, no matter how surprising, is true.

I can assert this because they emerged at two different moments during my evangelical activity as a missionary, the first during the years I spent in the Amazon jungle of Peru, and the second during my mission period on the island of Cuba.

The first story ("Pandemic"), which I originally titled "Without Quarantine," was conceived one afternoon in July 1998. Even today, I am amazed by how it happened. I sat in front of an old mechanical Remington typewriter at the parish house in Pevas on the banks of the Amazon. It was around five o'clock, and I did not stop until close to midnight, when I finished the entire story. Obviously, it had all sorts of flaws and errors, but the plot was clear and complete.

In fact, I experienced an incredible emotion and immense satisfaction when I finished. Perhaps, it's what it feels like to give birth to a firstborn.

The second emerged during those nights of solitude and isolation in the spring of 2006, which I lived through frequently over the two years I was on the paradisiacal Caribbean island. Also, while in Cuba, cockroaches nibbled at my nearly non-existent hair. This was something I discovered and was more frequent in the Amazon. This peculiar habit of these creatures was what motivated me to fantasize and reflect on the way of life, not just of them, but of all living beings.

Both stories are an excellent pretext to share my reflections on various themes that seem fundamental and of great significance to me. But above all, they have provided me with extraordinary solace and amusement.

Both are based on "REAL-LIFE EVENTS," although it is also true that the plot and its development are colored by my particular way of perceiving reality beyond simple daily facts.

"PANDEMIC" is topical (which is why I changed its title) and with a writing from twenty-two years ago, I try to give a one hundred eighty-degree turn to the perception that surely, through advertising, they have sold us to "die of fear," not of laughter.

"A CONSPIRACY" was initially named "cockroach-esque," as everything revolves around their malevolent plans. However, it's not necessary to attribute such intentions to another species of creation; some among us could surely attempt it.

I hope that you enjoy reading them as much as I enjoyed writing them. Similarly, if possible, may they serve to spark your interest in topics that I consider worthwhile.

PANDEMIC
(OR THE JOY OF SMILING)

LITERALLY

I'm dying of laughter! Ah! How many times have I said this? And never as true as today. It's literal, I'm dying of laughter. The way it happened was very strange and subtle. Perhaps, we don't realize how dangerous smiles can be when they are not remedied in time. I'll try to explain this.

I'm aware that I neglected myself, and that's why I'm dying because of them. You might wonder how I got into this situation. Well, I'll try to answer.

It was so long ago, so I'm sure I'll miss some details, but I'll try to be as faithful to the facts as possible.

THE BEGINNING

I remember it was one of those nights when I stayed up meditating in the living room. Several years had passed since I began practicing this discipline. The procedure was actually quite simple, as it involved sitting completely still for at least twenty minutes in the darkness. That's what I was doing, just like many other times, especially when I could be at the parish.

I remember that night, everyone was asleep. I sat in one of the armchairs in the usual manner and started with the basic relaxation exercises. As usual, it didn't take long for me to hear the "*tunchis*" (*tunchis* are part of the jungle beliefs, spirits that, although not necessarily evil, because they belong to another order of existence, do cause fear among the Amazonians). In reality, these were the normal sounds of a house built entirely of wood, but along with them, I noticed something that I initially identified as rats. It had been several days since I last heard them, as night after night, for a week, I had prepared them sumptuous dinners laced with "Champion" poison, so they had disappeared. Well, now I realized that it was only temporary.

Thanks to my attempt to stay in meditation, I managed to overcome the restlessness that thinking about the possibility of them suddenly bumping against my feet caused me. Thus, although the noises continued, I no longer paid them any attention.

Suddenly, I experienced a great startle. My heart was beating rapidly, and my pulse seemed like it was going to burst, but I remained still. I felt a flood of adrenaline coursing through my body, but still, I kept calm. I remained seated in complete rest. I definitely felt a slight touch on my right foot and, even with this, I remained unfazed—something I had never achieved before—in total stillness. It's also true that now I was attentive to the noises, and that's why I realized that those supposed rats were more than I thought, and they were moving very close to me. At that moment, I decided to move so they would get scared and end the "attack." I could hear them fleeing quickly, however, a sound caught my attention that was very different from their usual squeaking. It wasn't their characteristic squeal, as it was more like a murmur. Intrigued by this detail, I got up to end the meditation and go to sleep. Just like other times, I went to bed with the pleasant sensations that engulfed me after a good session of that activity, so I quickly fell asleep.

The next morning, during breakfast, I jokingly mentioned to the team that I needed to give the rats dinner again. Someone asked with some surprise why I made that comment. I told them about the events of the previous night, and all they said was that they hadn't heard them for a long time. Although it seemed strange to me, I made no further comments on the matter.

THE CONTAGION

I eagerly awaited nightfall to verify whether there truly were rats or if it was just my imagination.

A few minutes after the town plunged into darkness due to the power outage, and even more so in the living room of the house, which normally doesn't get much light (not even sunlight), I was sitting again in the armchair trying to meditate. I suppose I succeeded, as I didn't notice any noise. But I also don't recall having any images, sensations, or thoughts. It was like those occasions when the entire moment passed in a blank. Nor had I fallen asleep, since my body remained upright, unlike the times when the fatigue from a long day's activities prevented me from staying awake, and I could find myself slumped over with pain in my neck. It was only then that I felt something cling to my knee, causing me a great startle, but this time I had taken the precaution of placing a flashlight within reach, so I immediately grabbed it and, turning it on, directed the light towards what was clinging to me. My surprise was immense, for where I expected to find a rat in a threatening posture, I found a smile of beautiful whiteness.

There it was, with a look that could be defined as pleading and also showed a certain shyness. I could tell it had a friendly attitude, as it seemed to be seeking someone to welcome it. Given that it was strange for one of them to be near these regions and at this time of year, it still caused me fear. I remained looking at it without moving because I didn't want to scare it away, as I was convinced it was friendly and, moreover, having such a pet wouldn't be so bad. As it approached up my leg, I realized it was accompanied by a group of at least five more. All of them radiated whiteness, so I decided to lightly caress the first one, and that's when I noticed how the others gained confidence to come closer and play in my lap. I had to ensure they weren't too loud, as they might wake the other missionaries.

I was having so much fun that I no longer hesitated to accept and caress them; I felt we had become friends. Finally, after a fun time of smiles, I decided to go to bed, adopting the one that had approached me first. I made a little place for it between my lips and went to sleep with a smile on my face. That's how the contagion began.

BUSINESS AS USUAL

The next morning, I enjoyed the normal activities with a gesture of happiness on my face. For example, the smile discreetly appeared on my face during the exposition of the Blessed Sacrament, though at times it left me to go explore the place and meet the people I saw, but it immediately returned to continue brightening my countenance.

It seemed that no one noticed the first symptoms I was displaying of that contagion, or maybe they simply did not consider it important. I don't know, but the only thing someone mentioned was, "And now, why so happy? Why so smiley?" Apart from that comment, nothing happened that would show I had been infected with such a dangerous condition that manifests in happiness, joy, and delight. Even so, I noticed something that momentarily disturbed me, as I discovered it could reproduce quickly. I have no idea how this could be, since research in this field (as I understand) is still very rudimentary. The fact is that somehow the smiles were multiplying, and not only on my lips, but it momentarily seemed they began to fill others' as well.

I didn't pay much attention to that detail until days later, when I went out to bathe in the creek and started to notice that most people were smiling at me as they passed by. Then the suspicion began to grow within me that this was turning into an epidemic. Somehow, it comforted me to think that it wouldn't be bad to fall ill with an ailment like this; besides, I realized that if it were so, the most prone to contagion were the children, as I was sure they had not yet created antibodies against smiles, and in no time, a child could even emit loud and explosive laughter filled with transparent joy. It's also true that the town had never received a vaccine for this and would surely be easily infected, so it was to be assumed that soon we would be in the midst of a true pandemic. After thinking about that, I intensely enjoyed the bath at the end of the afternoon.

A PROBLEM

That afternoon, upon returning home, I found the team gathered and could notice a nervous smile on their faces, as well as some suspicion. They were worried since this was taking on the dimensions of a pandemic. Already some people—the most serious in the town—out of fear and even panic, as they were terrified of the idea of smiling naturally and joyfully, had notified the Ministry of Health with the intention of having them come to take control of the situation.

After deliberating for a while amidst laughter and guffaws, we decided to call the central house of the vicariate to see if they could send some remedy. We were informed that it was very difficult to obtain it from private institutions, that it was only available through the government (they are specialists in extinguishing smiles). The mission's guardian mentioned that there had been attempts to create a vaccine, but the scientists who tried to produce it failed, causing their experimental subjects to end up struck down by an attack of melancholy complicated with symptoms of deep depression.

Thus, we were left waiting for the authorities to take charge of the situation.

In some way, I felt very bad, as I knew that all of this had started by having accepted that smile as a pet. But, on the other hand, I realized that this broad, transparent, and sincere expression suited the people of the town very well. This contagion resembled malaria, which is chronically suffered by many in the jungle and yet they lead a relatively normal life. In the long run, they will surely come to die because of it, however, they can continue with their daily activities as normal.

GETTING WORSE

I felt that I was gradually weakening from the ailment, and although the rest of the team supposed they should encourage me, I understood that my illness was in a very advanced phase, as my hilarity had become completely spontaneous and I enjoyed the witty comments more and more, even if they weren't that funny. Smiles were a cascade flowing profusely not only from my lips but from my entire being. They had become a delightful perspiration that moistened me during the day and at night provided me with a benign freshness with a comforting warmth that filled me with peace. Another unmistakable symptom that I was reaching a critical state was manifested by the tremors, or perhaps I should say, the vibration that invaded my body when I got excited seeing children smile freely and without prejudice.

I feel that I am reaching the terminal phase of this contagion. I have stopped eating and cannot chew because the smile does not leave my lips. Although they have mentioned the possibility of feeding me through a tube, I have rejected it, as it would only unnecessarily prolong my agony. It is said in the town that my case is very peculiar, as it has never been known for someone to die of laughter. Well, but we know how towns are, something can be asserted and one never knows if it has a scientific basis. It is a fact that often it is about mere opinions or attempts to distort information for the benefit of a few.

THE SOLUTION

Several days have passed since the Ministry of Health was notified to address the issue, and today the arrival of the technicians who will try to solve the problem is expected. I can barely walk, but still, I want to go to the port, as the engine of the boat bringing the treatment to fight this epidemic can already be heard.

Supported on the shoulders of smiling children and surrounded by those who were infected because of me, I managed to reach the raft where a festive atmosphere with laughter reigned.

It was expected that the antidote brought by the Ministry of Health would be so effective, as soon as the head appeared with his stern, frowning face and something that is certainly nothing more than a semblance of a smile, many of those gathered there who had not been infected became very serious. Only those of us in advanced stages continued to radiate it freely. "Someone help unload the boxes," he shouted authoritatively.

"What's in those boxes?" asked the mayor.

"Prefabricated smiles," replied the person in charge.

Indeed, it could be read on the outside of each box: "LAUGHTER" and below: "The best quality." As if they were original. And although they were surely imitation, the legend "Made in USA" appeared. It was also significant that on the lid of each box, the logo of some national television network appeared as having donated it for "the noble cause" of combating the pandemic.

"Is this the antidote?" I asked.

The person in charge, accentuating his fake smile even more and with the air of an expert being interviewed, responded:

"Of course, the principle is simple, as these fake smiles are distributed among the population, and with that, they learn to laugh falsely, which causes the gradual disappearance of authentic smiles. Thanks to the fact that the prefabricated ones are totally controllable, they represent no danger to the population (nor to the government). While spontaneous and authentic smiles are free and uncontrollable, they become a serious risk of civil disorders—although the government will never admit this." Then, he gestured to one of the technicians accompanying him while saying:

"There's no time to waste; we have to distribute these smiles as soon as possible."

Immediately, each of the technicians displayed a wide smile (of course, prefabricated) and began distributing them to all those who were nearby.

At that precise moment, as I watched how that authentic and frank expression on people's faces changed to a stiff and deformed one, I was attacked by laughter, which caused me extreme weakness, and the last thing I remember is how some of the villagers, especially children, discreetly started to slip away. After that, I knew no more.

EVERYTHING UNDER CONTROL

Somehow, I ended up at the hospital in Iquitos, which has the necessary equipment to attend to almost anyone requiring general and specialized medical care. Someone from the parish team came to visit, and we have been talking about everything that happened in the town since I was transferred unconscious.

He has stepped out for a moment, as he went to bring the breviary so we can pray together.

The smile does not leave me; I believe I will die happy. The doctors said they rushed me here because my condition is terminal. Moreover, they want to study the case carefully, as they don't remember anything similar. Those who come to attend to me approach warily and always with masks on. Though I have occasionally noticed how a "discreet smile" is drawn on their lips. I suppose that at any moment they will start to experience the symptoms of the contagion, as some of them have attempted to joke with me about my state of health. Perhaps they do not realize, but I surely have already infected them.

I asked a visitor who arrived yesterday from the town about the situation there. He said seriously that "happily" everything was under control. At that moment, I felt that for the first time in a long time, and for a brief instant, joy disappeared from my lips; I thought that perhaps now the town would look very different, and although people had not stopped smiling, many were now doing it falsely.

The smile nested on my lips once more when I remembered the last thing I saw before fainting at the town's port and I said to myself: "Surely some (hopefully many) have been able to flee, in this way, at least a good number of them will be able to cause the whole town to become infected again in the future."

TRAGIC END

I believe that's how the events unfolded; I hope I have been faithful to the truth. That's why now I can literally say: "I'm dying of laughter! At this moment, I am surrounded by hundreds of them, fluttering around me, hopping from one side to the other, tickling me all over my body, and piling up on my lips. They fill the entire room with a radiant whiteness."

The laughter of those who have entered the room joins and merges with all these that come out of I don't know where. I'm sure that I am now saying goodbye with a wide, frank, clean, transparent, and simple smile that, with its winged whiteness, crosses the thresholds of this life to reach the One who is the Eternal Smile and who makes the entire universe smile with His infinite love.

Have you ever said: "I'm dying of laughter"? Be careful! Because if you don't quarantine, the next time you say it, it might be literal.

THE END

A CONSPIRACY
SPECIES SUPERIORITY

SLEEPING IN TACAJÓ

I guess it wasn't long after I had fallen asleep when I heard fluttering near my head. It wasn't unusual, as if it wasn't a moth trapped in the house, then it was one of those cockroaches that announce rain by fluttering everywhere. Although sharing the room with a bug like this wasn't pleasant, it also didn't keep me awake, since I've begun to accept their insolence, as recent scientific research has convinced us that they are one of the few species that would survive if a nuclear holocaust occurred. Perhaps that's why I hold respect for their kind, and not just for them but for any other living being, no matter how insignificant it may seem.

It didn't take me long to discover it was a cockroach, which was boldly tasting one of my very short hairs. Instinctively, I jumped out of bed (actually, it was a foam mattress thrown on the floor of the room) to rid myself of that unpleasant attack. Immediately, I grabbed the flashlight I always keep within reach on purpose. I assumed that would make it run away scared, however, I was greatly surprised when I saw it sitting on my pillow and, though it seems surprising and illogical, it had its leg crossed. I don't know if it was evident or just a hunch, but I sensed in it an attitude of defiance and arrogance.

I couldn't recover from my astonishment; I felt like I was in a Kafkaesque fantasy. I rubbed my eyes to erase that image, which I wanted to convince myself wasn't real. However, it not only didn't disappear but surprised me with something even more surrealistic, as it began to speak with a booming and awe-inspiring voice.

"Stop looking so stupid; it doesn't suit you at all," it sounded really confident as it pronounced these words. After what had happened before, this no longer surprised me, though it was very disconcerting. "Aren't you supposed to have an exceptionally open mind?" it continued.

"Where did you get that idea?" I illogically asked myself. I think it was right, as that's how I see myself. But blow after blow didn't allow me to recover from the first impact, from the shock; I had already become mute and so perplexed that I would have needed hours to recover from that shock.

"Alright," it said in a condescending voice. "I know I should apologize," it now started to sound genuine in its friendly attitude, which left me, if possible, even more surprised. "It's imprudent of me to present myself this way. After analyzing you carefully and thoroughly, I'm convinced that we are very much alike, but I understand you're bewildered to accept me as your equal," it continued. "You might be thinking you're going insane, and you're probably right, the same thing is happening to me. Since neither you nor I are even allowed to think about something of this nature, anyone of your species or mine who saw us now would surely judge us as crazy. Especially me, as they might allow me to talk with any other being of nature but, with a man, not even think about it. It's not that I have something personal against you or your kind," it seemed like it was apologizing. "It's just that only a deranged cockroach would try to talk with someone as despicable as a human being."

"What?! Hey!" I stammered clumsily trying to defend our species, but it completely ignored me.

"It would be inconceivable, yet I have dared; I hope I'm not mistaken."

A NEW SITUATION, YET ALL THE SAME

As he finished pronouncing these words, I became aware of something especially peculiar. I don't know if he had been growing or I was shrinking. Strangely, this did not cause me any fear, so docilely I was adapting to this new situation.

"I warn you," he resumed what he was saying earlier, adding a touch of mystery to his voice, "what you are about to witness must stay between us."

At that moment, I managed to observe him with a bit of calm. Now, his appearance seemed so human that I could perceive the color of his skin, his hair, his height, among other characteristics. However, I also wondered if it wasn't me who was taking on a cockroach-like appearance. Without realizing how, he had already passed his arm over my shoulder (or should I say my wing) and was guiding me through passageways and places I never imagined existed in my room.

Finally, we arrived at a very spacious area; it was a large cavern where hundreds of thousands of cockroaches were gathered. I had already experienced enough with his appearance to the degree that this did not cause me the slightest apprehension; however, it seemed very strange to me that no one was alarmed by my presence. I assumed that my mere human appearance must surprise everyone, and yet they continued with what they were doing. Only one or two glanced at us momentarily, perhaps believing they recognized someone or as a potential prospect for some business or transaction.

"Wait here for a moment."

He sentenced me and moved forward a few steps to open a small door that seemed like the backroom of a commercial establishment. I shrugged my shoulders in resignation, and he, winking at me, disappeared closing it behind him.

Out of nowhere, a voice that captured my attention emerged.

"I have what you need, how much do you want?" I heard behind me.

"What?!" I tried to ask, feeling greatly startled. "What is it about? I don't know what you're talking about. Need what?" As I turned to discover who was speaking to me, I spoke again.

I almost fainted from surprise upon discovering that the one speaking to me was very familiar. In front of me was another cockroach, which faithfully reflected the features of Juan Isidro, well, albeit with an evident cockroach-like appearance.

"Chilo..."

I hesitated, because although I reacted sure that the cockroach was Chilo and therefore had no qualms about greeting him effusively, at the same time, by instantly becoming aware that I was not in my world and that it could not be that dear friend, I stopped.

"Sorry?" I said, trying to react equanimously. "I didn't understand your question."

I spoke as if I had control of the situation, even though that wasn't possible. I changed my way of speaking, as I perceived he looked at me with total indifference, and even with contempt. This was not related to my human condition, as my appearance was that of a perfect cockroach. If I saw myself in a mirror, the same thing would happen to me, as I could discover my cockroach appearance, but still, my features were those of Alberto.

"I see you can't decide," I felt that phrase was more an attack than a statement, "or are you avoiding admitting you don't have 'money'" he continued while I looked into his eyes, only to feel the annoyance in his gaze, for although it seemed like Chilo's, he spoke to me in a functional and absent manner just like employees forced to work a schedule for a minimum wage and without incentives that motivate them to be more amicable with customers.

"You're right," I lied, trying to end that uncomfortable situation, "I don't carry money."

Then a look of annoyance appeared on his face, almost bordering on disdain or hatred, and without uttering a word, he turned around and disappeared around a nearby corner. I was again in shock when I heard:

"What are you up to?"

It was the voice of that cockroach who had returned to my side.

"Ah, ah, yes, I, well, I..." I couldn't quite pull myself together. "What's happening?" I managed to ask this question.

"You look perplexed," he said, staring at me intently, trying to penetrate my confused thoughts. "What happened to you?" he asked impatiently but trying to instill some of the calm I so desperately needed.

"I don't know, I really don't know," I replied while trying to organize my thoughts. "It was exactly like Chilo," I didn't really know what I was saying; it was more of a catharsis than an answer.

"What are you talking about?" he growled impatiently, "you're not explaining, and I don't understand you," he said, clearly annoyed.

"Let's leave it at that," I said decisively and feeling totally helpless. "What comes next?" I surprised myself with the serenity with which I could respond.

"Since there are no further comments," he tried to change the subject, "let's go, my friends are already waiting for us," he said as naturally as if it were the most familiar thing to me.

"Ah! Yes, your friends," I implied irony in my words. "I forgot about them, what are their names?"

Of course, I had no idea if they could be called by a proper name.

"They are called..." I made a rhetorical pause, as if asking him to remind me of the name, at least of one. He remained silent while we began to walk. I could notice that he looked at me with a mix of perplexity and disdain, with doubt, as if saying, "Don't play the fool." He shook his head in resignation as he ordered me to be quiet and to keep walking. "Well, at least I have the right to know what all this is about. You took me out of my world without asking, I feel like I've been kidnapped. I know it's not like that, but that's my impression," I took on a submissive attitude. "Could you at least tell me why I am here?"

THE DOCK

(Between Fiction and Reality)

Though he didn't physically do it, it was as if he had covered my mouth, for at that moment we had entered a small underground room where at least half a dozen cockroaches were waiting for us. Of course, I should have been surprised, but by this point, I had become so accustomed to surprises that I thought nothing could unsettle me anymore. I couldn't accurately describe that scene, as it resembled a council or a jury in deliberative session where the individuals were seated, except for one, who seemed so elderly that he couldn't stand being in those uncomfortable chairs for long, even for their anatomy.

Then it dawned on me that I was about to be judged by this cockroach tribunal. So much so, there was a small bench.

"It can't be!" I thought to myself. They are going to sit me on that "dock" of the accused, and I don't even know what my crime is. At that moment, it seemed plausible that I had been kidnapped to be judged for violating some law of their peculiar world. Suddenly, thousands of images from those movies that seemed ridiculous to me (now I wasn't so sure about that) where insects take over the planet and the first thing they do is avenge the damages humans have caused them, flashed through my mind. As I lived (perhaps I should say: endured) this scene and that whirlwind of ideas and thoughts raced through my head, I felt a shiver run down my body and my scalp tingle with what I suppose could be called fear.

That was what I was feeling at that moment, so I cast a look of distress and plea at my friend (could I call him that?), who in turn looked at me, dispelling my fears without really knowing why.

"Come on, take a seat," he whispered to me, "don't be afraid, I assure you it's not what you think." I couldn't help but stare at him intently, now without the pressure of thinking my life was in danger.

It was then I realized that the face of that cockroach seemed very familiar. I could think it was because I was getting used to seeing him, however, I discovered that wasn't the reason.

"Of course!" I exclaimed inwardly. "It's 'Lencho'" —well, it was the cockroach version of Lorenzo Valenzuela. Even the tone of his voice and his grave and benevolent gaze suited him well.

"Gentlemen," said my friend "Lencho" in a solemn tone. By then, I was seated, "I present to you Alberto, of whom I have spoken so much" —I noticed an atmosphere of expectation and charged with emotions. It seemed to be a moment long awaited by that peculiar group—. "It hasn't been difficult to bring him here, although I must say he seems very bewildered. That's why I believe it's essential that we give him an explanation of what this is all about" —those words made me feel I wasn't wrong to consider this "Lencho" as a friend—. "I suggest," he continued, "that Don Jesús should provide our guest with some context" —without a doubt, it seemed normal to me that this cockroach individual had the traits of "Don Chuchito".

"So?" I whispered to my friend with a gesture for him to come closer. "Surely you are Valenzuela" —he looked at me with great astonishment and nodded, but without saying a word and signaling me to keep quiet.

"What do you think of my proposal?" said Lencho. Although there was no vote or anything like that, the group's consent was palpably felt.

"Ahem!" Don Chuchito cleared his throat. "Firstly, and on behalf of all my companions, I want to apologize for the way you've ended up here. I can assure you that this is not a kidnapping and, though it all may appear to be a tribunal, believe me, nothing could be further from the truth."

It was as if I was listening to the voice of Don Jesús himself, who was known for that quiet and measured way of speaking that led many to assume he had limited intellectual capacity. However, those of us who know him are witnesses to his privileged intelligence capable of dazzling anyone, even considering that he has recently suffered from Parkinson's, which has accentuated that appearance. His lucidity, in reality, has not been affected at all.

"We have deliberated a lot about this meeting," these words brought me back to the discourse of the cockroach Don Jesús. "All this has meant a significant economic investment; in addition to efforts, battles of ideas and opinions, as well as a great number of hours and dialogues at all levels to reach an agreement on the advisability of this project."

By the way he handled the data, it gave me the impression that the respectable Don was the heart of this whole entanglement in which I found myself involved.

"It is a fact that we have come to this moment through our own means. By the initiative of a small group interested in finding the best way to harmonize the various realities of our world."

I couldn't believe it! It was like listening to a diplomatic speech at the United Nations or in one of those international forums that always leave the impression of being empty. At the same time, I tried to place myself in the fact that I was in the midst of a seemingly super-advanced society of cockroaches and that I didn't even know why it was me, precisely, who was here listening to the words of this wise cockroach, who, by the way, does not seem (appearances can deceive) in the least bit wanting to harm me. On the contrary, he seemed more interested in seeking a friendly relationship.

"Now that, moreover," he continued with that touch of severity he had adopted from the beginning, "if we had waited for the governments to come to some agreement, we would never have reached this point in the project."

What I was hearing made me suppose that they were part of a highly organized society, yet not really efficient, and that they could be considered dissidents.

"First of all, and to make it clear, everything that involves being in this dialogue places us at the limits between reality and fiction. Let me explain," he said in response to my look of doubt and skepticism, which, thanks to his keen intuition, he had noticed in me. "We can say that it is real that members of this privileged and superior society are in communication with you, who represent a species as insignificant and despicable as the human one."

Again, I heard that assertion which had been so annoying to me from the start and which now, although it still bothered me, I was beginning to accept.

"It is real, for we have created a type of transcription not only of our language and mode of communication but also of the categories, parameters, and referents of our civilization, culture, and society to yours."

What he said seemed clear, but it ventured into a territory beyond the fields of logic, philosophy, science, and, if possible, also theology. I could not imagine, even though I intuited, how he was going to harmonize all these levels, not just of reflection, but of living, of experience, and of being into which he was delving.

"In reality, at this moment, all of us," he continued, "are under the action of an interface that we have agreed to call 'Interespeciatic Audioconceptual Perception System' (IAPS)."

KILLING COCKROACHES

At that moment, he made a gesture with his eyes and a prearranged sign, which caused me to be abruptly pulled from that environment. Like in a whirlwind, my surroundings dissolved into a nonsensical collage. Suddenly, I could barely open my eyes and peek into an alternate reality light-years away. I could dimly make out a small group of cockroaches on the floor of my room while I sat on the edge of my bed. With my legs crossed in half lotus and a feeling of indecision, with the flashlight in my left hand and a sandal in the other.

In my mind echoed the question: "What am I trying to achieve?"

Certainly, I have no reason to kill them. They are not attacking me in any way, nor are they a threat. True, they repulse me, and likewise, I find it very unpleasant to think that while I sleep, they might crawl over my body and nibble on me. But even that I can endure. If I were to act solely based on that aversion, I would promptly finish them off, as there's nothing stopping me, not a single civil law that would penalize me for it. Perhaps, I might feel some guilt for ending a living being's life. However, I've learned to live with that.

Yet, on the other hand, it's true that I always need to ask myself if it makes sense to end the existence of such insignificant, defenseless, and inferior beings just because I am superior to them. At that moment, I reflected on my indecision being due to my certainty that life, in any of its forms, deserves respect no matter how insignificant it may seem. The hesitation was quite unbearable due to the fact of being there in front of those cockroaches, unsure if I was thinking this or hallucinating. Even amidst that confusion, I could glimpse my deeper motivations about the value of all that lives.

Related to this, I've come to the conviction that if we dare dispose of a defenseless life just because we consider ourselves superior or because we won't suffer any sanction, we prove ourselves to be murderers. Perhaps many wish to end a human being's life, however, the legal burden that such an act entails is what prevents the vast majority from deciding to exterminate another. When an individual has convinced themselves that there are human beings inferior to others and manages to convince the authority so that no sanctions are applied, they wouldn't hesitate to murder. Then almost any reason would suffice to erase them from the face of the earth. Perhaps it is the case of some individuals throughout human history who do not accept the equality of people and have managed to convince others, so the limits that could prevent them from exterminating those they consider inferior disappear.

Surely it is the case of genocides, like the overly publicized one of the Jews. Also, that of China, which was the country in Asia that suffered the most at the hands of the Japanese during the so-called Second Sino-Japanese War from 1937 to 1938 and World War II from 1939 to 1945. The same as the one that occurred in America, perpetrated by the Spanish, English, and Portuguese. All of them from the past but, just like in our time, abortion policies and countless exterminations are based on the idea of the superiority of some over others. Thus, the destruction of life is attempted to be justified by implanting criteria of a system that worships death.

"Is this what I want to attempt?" I was still in my room, questioning myself internally while extending my hand with the sandal in it to deliver a killing blow to that crowd of despicable and insignificant insects. The action was almost automatic and easy to conclude. Perhaps some of them could have escaped, but it was at that precise moment when they transformed again into the peculiar council that was subjecting me to scrutiny, and once more, I found myself enveloped in that cockroach environment from which I had been torn moments ago.

"Alright, thank you for the demonstration," I heard Don Jesús's voice as he addressed these words to someone I couldn't see, somewhere in the darkness of the room. "You surely clearly perceived the effect of the IAPS."

I listened to his voice, yet I was unsure if I fully grasped what had just happened.

WHAT IS THE "IAPS" DOING TO ME?

"What happened to me?" I managed to ask, looking around me, unable to shake off my daze. It felt as if I had passed out and lived through a hallucination. Although, on second thought, I could no longer distinguish between reality and illusion. "I don't understand what's happening to me" —now I was asking for someone to take pity on me and clarify everything.

"Don't worry," I heard the voice of a new cockroach. "We understand you feel so bewildered. What happened is that we momentarily disconnected you from the IAPS" —the voice sounded very professional and capable of using any kind of technical language. "Sorry," he apologized, "I haven't introduced myself."

Of course, it wasn't necessary, because just by looking at him, I could suppose it was Isidoro. He was sitting with his leg crossed and carefree as someone who masters the situation, exactly like that brother priest so close in ministerial life. That strange cockroach gaze and so much of Lolo reflected the experience of someone who had made his way through life and ministry on his own. Also, the neatness of his clothes and the fragrance that could be sensed even from meters away.

These traits perhaps contrasted, without clashing, with his way of facing life always in a critical key and with a strong accent of subversion, dissatisfaction, and rebellion. It wasn't hard to perceive in his meticulously cared for and polished shoes a discreet taste for the refined. This aspect of his image went hand in hand with his empathy towards the discriminated, marginalized, and undervalued.

"I am Isidoro," he said kindly, which pleased me because I hadn't been mistaken. "I am in charge of the continuous monitoring of the IAPS."

Don Jesús's figure had faded into the background, now my interlocutor was this cockroach version of Lolo.

"I've taken the liberty of speaking because I believe it's necessary for you to understand a little better how we came to create this system of intercommunication between different species," I knew I was about to hear a lecture on scientific cosmology along with logic and epistemology.

"Wait a moment," I interrupted Lolo's speech. "Don Jesús said we're bordering the limits between reality and fiction," with these words, I picked up the thread of the previous exposition to connect it with this new intervention by Lolo. "I can understand that we are really conversing and that this tribunal, or whatever we want to call it, does exist, but what guarantees me that what I perceive is not just a hallucination and that at any moment I can become aware of my true existence, and thus all this would become just an absurd fantasy, or a bad dream."

"Well, what happens is..." I noticed Lolo hurried to give an explanation. However, it was imperative for me to cover my ears with my hands, for at that precise moment a deafening noise erupted, making every brick of the place that housed us vibrate. Even the ground trembled under my feet. Amid that din, a new panel of lights lit up, dazzling me with their brightness; they were so powerful that I could discern that the place we were in was nothing but a stage where they attempted (not to deceive me) to make the sophisticated device required by the IAPS more user-friendly to me. Simultaneously, a number of alarms sounded, their flashing lights and multicolored indicators driving me mad.

"Don't let him go!" a voice coordinated the technical team responsible for the routines and subroutines of that interspecies system through loudspeakers. "We're losing him!" This last phrase faded in my ears because, just like before, I started to experience the sensation of dizziness that had torn me from this environment. "Don't let him go!" I could faintly hear the repetition of the desperate command.

That was the last thing I perceived from that cockroach world before feeling my eyes slightly open in my room, awakened by the deafening sound of the whistle from Tacajó's central mill, signaling it was two-thirty in the morning (the time for the night shift change). I realized that it was this sound that was waking me up in darkness as it had many times at the beginning, then I became so accustomed to it that I no longer even heard it while I slept. The awakening was so brief and sudden that it practically didn't register in my memory, because after my blink, the entire elaborate interspecies system appeared before me once more.

"We have him back," I heard at the same time as all the commotion caused by the mill's whistle faded away. "We can continue!" said the voice coordinating the team again.

Now my mind felt numb, unable to think or feel anything. I looked around with a deep sense of alienation.

"Do you feel okay?" I heard Lolo's voice.

I wanted to respond, but I couldn't, nor did I have the slightest intention to do so. I simply looked at him and glanced over every one of the attendees.

"This isn't bad at all," I said to myself. "I'm going back and forth between two entirely different worlds and can maintain, at least partially, the awareness of both. Yet, it's just a hallucination" —with this thought, I tried to convince myself of that fact.

"Alberto, do you feel okay?" Lolo insisted.

I was almost smiling and inexplicably felt like I was floating in the middle of that room. Along with this, all worry related to this surreal experience had vanished.

I began to understand that there might be a much deeper link not only between these two worlds but throughout our entire universe. So, if we got used to considering this diversity, we could achieve harmony with our own world, dimension, or reality (however we conceive it) with what has existed, exists, and even might come to exist. I was experiencing a sensation that filled me with peace, to the point that explanations about this commotion they had organized in my honor were almost unnecessary.

"No, I'm not okay," I replied, waiting for Lolo's worried reaction.

"What's wrong? Does something hurt?" he asked, not hiding his distress and concern.

"I'm not just okay, I'm exceptionally well," I finished the first part of my response.

"Phew! You had us worried," he said as his body language reflected immense relief. "It's clear you're okay now;

you've gone back to your bad habit of joking like that," he spoke as if he were the same Lolo who knows me well and who has inevitably suffered from my situational humor. I call it that because it arises according to the moment and is not based on pre-established jokes or pranks.

THEY DON'T KNOW WHO THEY'RE DEALING WITH

By this point, I had recovered and was as confident as if I were in my own environment.

"I don't think I'm evading," I said as I resolutely stood up from my seat. "You haven't finished telling me in what sense all this is at the same time real and fictional," I said straightforwardly to Don Jesús, noticing the confusion and concern my new attitude was causing. "I believe I've understood, at least in general terms, what the IAPS means," with these words, I was revisiting the topic that this interspecies experience lies at the limits between reality and fiction. "However, I haven't quite understood why this can be considered fiction," I concluded my questioning, and everyone turned their gaze towards Don Jesús.

"Alright," he took the floor again. "If you realize, this cannot be entirely real," I felt he was starting to complicate things, as for me, there was no difficulty in accepting that all this was happening. "Well, or at least," he conceded, "we cannot be entirely sure that we are establishing an authentic communication between our species," he made a brief pause as if to allow me to ponder over his last statement. "As far as we are concerned, we don't know if you are capable of coherently formulating a holistic understanding of the universe."

This time I was not willing to stay silent in the face of this suspicion that was irritating me so much.

"Hold on, hold on," I interrupted his speech, showing annoyance in my voice. "I want to clarify something that I'm not liking at all," I continued. "I'm tired of being judged as an inferior species by you. Haven't you considered that perhaps it's you who are the inferiors?" Everyone's gaze was fixed on me, showing great astonishment, as they apparently did not expect me to have the capacity to hold a debate like this with them. "Why don't you consider the basis of your claim of superiority?" At this moment, I noticed clear skepticism on every face. "Do you think you're superior to us because you've developed a sophisticated system that allows communication between species?" I said, growing more confident in controlling the situation, especially since I was beginning to employ one of my favorite weapons, rhetoric. "Haven't you considered that perhaps we have everything needed to create those kinds of interfaces?" As I continued with my dissertation, discreet snickers of mockery could be heard, which they perhaps considered entirely absurd. "And that, maybe, we are not giving you enough importance to try to communicate with you."

Now everyone listened attentively, as it seemed that this last argument could be considered valid.

"Furthermore, and finally," I resumed my defense, "both you and us, in trying to prove who is superior to whom, only demonstrate that we are nothing more than species that have not managed to harmonize, neither with our interspecies environment nor with other beings of nature."

Definitely, they were now listening to me, and I was becoming as assertive as to cause rejection in my audience, which could lead my interlocutor to dismiss my arguments outright, ignoring me, or alternatively, to side with me without questioning anything and, consequently, without benefit to either party.

"I would like to explain myself as best as possible," I said next, fearing to make them feel bad. "I think I understand and am capable of accepting that you consider us inferior. However, if we take into account the fact that until now, if it weren't for your IAPS, we couldn't understand the cultural entirety of other species," I resumed the attack. "Realize that human beings could have thought exactly the same about you because, ignorant of your cultural context, we did not imagine that, although incomprehensible to us from many different aspects, your world is coherent and worthy of being considered a fully civilized and developed society."

WE'VE ALWAYS BEEN DOMINATED

A new character entered the scene.

"All that's well and good as a speech," intervened Nore. "But you're not going to convince me with that philosophical trifle."

There was no doubt about it, this cockroach had to be named Norberto, whom we liked to call Nore. His stereotypical cultured man's gesture, the arrogance that betrayed a fundamental insecurity, his glassy, jittery gaze that denoted hidden nervousness, his meticulous dissertations aimed at checkmating all his discussions; all of it revealed his cunning, as well as his lack of reflective capacity. I couldn't be mistaken, it was Nore.

"I'd like you to answer the following," he was now about to challenge me. "How do you explain that throughout your entire history you haven't been able to rid yourselves of even one of our attacks, so harmful to you?" He indeed made me open my mouth in astonishment.

"Sorry?" I asked, puzzled. "I don't understand what you're referring to, Nore." Now it was his turn to open his eyes wide in surprise because I pronounced his name, even without supposing that I would know him. "What do you mean you've been continuously attacking us?" I clarified my question. "Are you referring to the fact that you have been continuously invading our home environments with such arrogance?" I said, trying to fully understand his point. No sooner had I finished my question than a clear laugh from my scrutineers sounded.

"Please," Nore naturally imbued his voice with irony. "Don't make us laugh," he said, finishing recomposing his voice after his boisterous laugh. "No, man, no; those are reckless tourists looking for extreme experiences for fun, adrenaline addicts, risking their lives attempting to return and recount the thrill of being attacked and surviving (though not all do). Of course, that's not it," he clarified, intending to bring the seriousness required back to the conversation. "It doesn't even come close to being significant in our society," he walked a few steps in front of me, as always, giving himself great importance trying to convince us he dominated the subject he was now about to address. "Haven't you thought about why you live increasingly far from nature, that an ever larger part of the world population is isolating and crowding into urban environments that destroy them without their realization, and, despite this, do nothing to live more naturally, which would bring them fulfillment?"

Listening to him, I realized he was right. By mentioning our irrational behavior in that regard, he justified classifying us as inferior.

"No, I hadn't thought of that," I said, a bit flustered. "Maybe, I could attribute it to our immediacy that makes us forget what is fundamental and transcendent," I finished my response.

"It seems very reasonable what you say," Nore admitted. "It even seems very philosophical, and why not, also theological, however, you'll be surprised how immediate and pragmatic the answer is," he left me open-mouthed again, because now I feared I was about to hear something very unpleasant for my already quite disturbed human sensitivity. "Well," he began. "Do you remember when you used to wear your hair minimally long?" I nodded. "You'll also remember the countless times you woke up at night feeling like one of us seemed to be nibbling your hair?" Once more, I nodded. "Well, in reality, it wasn't a culinary attack, but since the margin left by your hair was so small, it wasn't possible for us to install an interface designed to convince you that the best way of life you could aspire to was away from nature. This device requires the hair to be at least two millimeters long to be installed and function correctly. The moment you reached that hair length limit, it was very difficult for us to install it, so our attempts were very frequently frustrated. Every time you realized it was because it had not been possible to complete the operation, thus, you've been escaping our suggestion. If you think about it, the shortness of your hair coincides with your increasingly clear conviction that living in contact with nature and away from cities is the best way to live."

I felt like I was in a quagmire without arguments to counter my interlocutor.

"Well," Nore continued, "the vast majority of people look for ways not to lose their hair, or at least they do not adapt to wearing it too short, and for us, that is very convenient, as it is the most effective means to induce thoughts and attitudes directly into the cerebral cortex" —this was too much, I felt that although I had no arguments to refute him, I was not going to accept this humiliation to which our species was being subjected without question. "But you might wonder: why are we interested in causing such a suggestion?" he said, as I saw a mocking smirk on the faces of the other cockroaches at my bewilderment.

WE ARE JUST CATTLE!

"Let me tell you that the reason for this effort is because humans who are subjected to stress situations, that is, feelings of dissatisfaction, frustration, discouragement, depression, and hatred for long periods, activate a series of neurohormonal, neuronal, and neurotrophic processes that generate a wide range of substances, including hormones (especially cortisol and adrenaline), which they leave scattered everywhere through their natural secretions, or that, when they die, go directly into the ground, where we harvest them."

As I listened to this, I felt like I was sinking into a foul pit that made me nauseous; I wanted to get out of there and take a breath of fresh air, but I overcame this impulse thinking it was better to fully understand it, as it would surely be beneficial for me.

"These substances," he almost rubbed his words in my face, "are not nutritional sources for us." I thought for a moment he would give me good news, however, I sensed I was about to hear something even worse. "To feed, their corpses, which they generously provide in cemeteries, suffice for us, not to mention the food waste they produce in industrial quantities all around the globe, which, by the way, they are unique in the art of wasting raw materials of all kinds."

It was true; the opinion that not only cockroaches but also other species of nature had of us couldn't be worse. I almost felt ashamed in front of that tribunal which, although not wanting to judge me, made me aware of things I had not considered before.

"In reality," Nore continued, "the reason we are interested in those substances is because they accumulate, in their basic form, in our genetic structures simply by coming into contact with them, and that is precisely what has made us one of the few species resistant to nuclear radiation and that will eventually save us from extinction in the not too distant future."

"So," now I could articulate words to ask, "is that the reason why even among us you have earned the reputation of being resistant to extinction, at least due to a nuclear apocalypse?"

"That's right, in addition to many other reasons for extinction," added Nore. "This is something we do not want humans to know, but it has inevitably leaked out in some way, and precisely for that reason, we have taken the initiative to have this meeting with you," concluded Nore, who with a reverent gesture passed the word to Don Jesús.

GLIMPSES OF HOPE

Don Jesús, cleaning his glasses, said: "Why did we ask Lencho to bring you here?" he posed rhetorically. "First of all, we would like to apologize through you to all of your species because, as you rightly asserted, neither you nor we have achieved sufficient harmony to coexist peacefully with all beings of nature. We would like to understand your civilization well enough to seek new ways of coexistence between our species."

"To tell the truth," Don Jesús continued, "until now we were not sure if you could be considered an advanced species," now he spoke as if to himself. "And as you mentioned earlier, only after this contact can we properly review our stance towards you," he said while directing his gaze at the other members of the scrutinizing team. "We have had countless debates about whether it was worth it, and until now, the majority claimed it was futile to deal with you." Again, I heard that annoying assertion, but this time I realized the topic was taking a very different direction.

"I suppose that, from now on," he sighed, as if seeing something very valuable lost, "our way of seeing you will be very different."

"And tell me about it," I interrupted with a rhetorical question to show that I felt the same about them. It was true that now I could no longer see them in the same way, not because they had the appearance of people close to me, but because what I had remotely intuited about the equal value of all living beings and nature could now become in me a certain conviction.

"How do you think I feel about you?" I dared to question, already with an attitude of total openness to interspecies dialogue. "I would like to clear up a doubt," I began to formulate the question.

GOD HAS MADE US SUPERIOR

"What do you base your conviction of superiority over other species on?" I actually expected an answer that I already knew. "Let me say," I began an explanation of my question, "that from the beginnings of our civilization, we have resorted to various discourses and reflections at all levels of knowledge and experience in order to convince ourselves that we are the beings at the pinnacle of creation. We handle all sorts of claims, from those that are scientific or claim to be, to the most religious; in fact, these latter are the ones that most easily generate the illusion of being the most advanced species, at least on our planet. Only a few individuals," I said, trying to sufficiently clarify the point, "throughout history have escaped the temptation to resort to divine revelation to affirm our superiority as a species."

I remembered Francis of Assisi, who considered all beings of creation as equals in dignity, including inanimate beings. Also others who, throughout history, have been judged as crazy because they dared to propose that all beings of creation are equal. Also coming to my mind are all those who fight against anti-life initiatives because they have understood that this treasure is found in all beings of creation, even those we consider inanimate. This is because each and every one of the created beings expresses the same vital current that flows throughout the universe. But it's also true that we have isolated ourselves within our conceptual or species-specific limits, or whatever we want to call them, to such an extent that we have lost the ability to sniff out the trail of life, wherever it may be found.

"It would seem," I started to propose, "that the issue of the superiority of one species over others is a concern of individuals who have not opened themselves to the concert of created beings, where each and every one harmonizes with the others their particular way of manifesting the life that flows in them," I said more as a reflection for myself. "I suppose that at some moments in the development of vital energy, the interaction of different species in the same time and space causes an apparent advantage or disadvantage among them, which produces the fantasy of dominance or superiority of one over the other," I continued my reflection. "However, what really happens in those moments, is that one of them has become the oblation element in the equation, while the other becomes the beneficiary in this exchange or interaction of the game of life. Lastly," I said to conclude, "I would dare to say that, fundamentally, this whole topic is the projection of a collective arrogance of our species."

"INTERSPECIES" HARMONY

"Perhaps you have an experience similar to ours," I continued with another question.

Nore, raising the volume of his voice, said, "But don't you realize the absurdity of what you're saying? It's inconceivable that someone would question that we are the species chosen by God to dominate the earth and subdue it." That way of speaking sounded familiar to me. "Our sacred text clearly states we were created as cockroaches with the noble purpose of being the Lords of this world. We have been granted the privilege of the cockroach avatar, making us a lineage of God."

"Hold on, Nore," Isidoro interrupted. "Let me remind you that we've discussed this before, and if at one time we couldn't boast of such a thing, even less after listening to Alberto," Lolo looked at me, and now I could perceive acceptance in his gaze, something that previously seemed impossible. "And, at its time and by the way," Lolo sentenced with those phrases that characterized him so much, "we can see that it's an unsustainable stance, very inconsistent and, therefore, we shouldn't even mention it."

Nore clenched his teeth in impotence, as his attempt to vindicate his species as the most perfect beings of creation seemed to be frustrated again.

"What happens," Nore said as he went to take his place again, "is that in this council, divine revelation has not been taken seriously, and that's why we've lost ground in the divine privilege of dominating the world." With these words, he closed his mouth without expecting further participation.

"I think you were saying something interesting about the arrogance of species," Lolo resumed the topic. "How do you frame the issue?" he asked.

"I don't really know," it was a rhetorical hesitation on my part. "In our world, we understand that there is divine revelation and, just as Nore mentioned, we affirm that God has descended into our human history to give us a privileged position in the world; we conclude this from God's very act of creation," I was engaging in theology. "However, I was saying that some individuals have come to interpret with a clear vision that this privilege is nothing but an illusory fantasy resulting from our need for self-affirmation, which in turn stems from a clearly immature attitude."

Were these words really coming out of my mouth? I wasn't even sure if I had reflected on this before or if it was the result of the IAPS influencing me, causing an altered state of consciousness, making it possible for me to see clearly enough reasons for such a stance.

"So, if we could overcome this immaturity, we would realize that we deceive ourselves when we claim to be the owners of creation. Thus, these visionaries understand that God does not ask us to dominate anyone on earth, but invites us to join in a single universe where the pulse of life can be felt in all its fullness."

As I uttered these words, I could experience the emotion I live when preaching. Similarly, I felt I had established contact with my audience and that I could make them see things they had not considered before.

"In fact," I picked up the topic again, "the clearest avatar for many of us," I was quoting Nore's earlier participation, "is Christ and, perhaps if we understood his message well, we would understand that he taught us how to dominate the world, but not by oppressing others, but by serving them to bring forth life in the universe through the total giving of one's own existence. This is not the concept of domination we all know. It seemed like Christ was at a disadvantage when he gave his life for everyone. Many even supposed that by dying on the cross, he had been crushed like a cockroach, I say this with all due respect," I clarified unnecessarily. "In my world, it's just a way of speaking. However, with that extreme oblation, he showed us how each individual and each species can relate harmoniously with other beings of nature."

Was I dreaming or hallucinating? Did this truly have the coherence of a wise reflection springing from me without my realizing it?

"In the individual realm," I continued, "each being decides whether to give their life for others or to shut themselves in their individualism and die, causing signs of death in their surroundings. Similarly, it seems to me that in the concert of species, they would have to decide which side of the equation they wish to belong to. In our interspecies conflict," I said with great determination, "I suppose that the one capable of more oblativity will triumph or be superior," was I really saying this? "That is, the one that is willing to give itself for the other to convey life. In the same sense, the defeated species would be the one that locks itself in its own world and seeks to keep itself alive only to actually die."

A nearly contemplative silence took over the scrutinizing committee. Their gazes were fixed on some non-existent point, except for Nore's, who was drumming his fingers against his mouth in a sign of total disapproval.

"Honestly, I'm not capable of engaging in discussions like this," Lencho broke the silence. "But it's clear to me what Alberto is saying, and I know we can accept it." The attitude of this cockroach version of Lencho was identical to his human counterpart.

"That is, we cannot claim any privilege over other species," he continued, while comfortably seated but with an attentive and serenely listening posture. "I think it's necessary to open ourselves to the possibility," he reflected with his eyes closed in an attitude of deep meditation, "that in reality, it's too presumptuous of us, and I suppose of any species, to claim that something or someone has made us the pinnacle of creation's beings."

I turned to look at Lencho, who had dropped those words into the middle of the council like a monolith that simply can be contemplated. That moment was brief but intense and profound.

"However," Don Jesús now intervened, resuming his speech interrupted moments before, "all this is true and really valuable, but I must tell you that we have very little influence on our world to change our stance towards you," I remembered that he had been apologizing for using us disrespectfully for the purpose of survival. "Since we are just a small group of dissenters trying to change our approach to the human species, it's not possible to assure you that things will change from now on. However, I'm sure that we can increasingly understand the role we have in the cosmos, and thus we will become the most oblationary part of the equation."

I noticed again that gesture and almost imperceptible signal he directed to the hidden IAPS team, so I hurried to say:

"Imagine the position you're putting me in, to go back with a story like this, and to already have what it takes to be considered a lunatic. I suppose there's very little or nothing I can do to influence how we think of you in our world. However, I promise you two things: first, that I will keep my hair short so that I continue loving nature, and second, that I will never perceive you the same way again. Even though you may provoke some repulsion in me, I'll try not to squash you just because."

THANK GOD, JUST A DREAM (?)

I could barely utter these last words as I once again felt myself being ripped away from that cockroach environment and reintegrated into my own, into my room illuminated by the first rays of the sun. I felt the urge to give thanks to God; first of all, for a new day, and second, because I now realized that everything I had experienced in the world of cockroaches was nothing but a dream (or should I say: a nightmare).

I could feel happy, as now in my room everything looked as normal as always, moreover, there were no traces of cockroaches anywhere. So, after taking a bath (brrr, so cold!) —by the way, it's not my custom... haha, just kidding— I headed to the kitchen to make myself a coffee, as this is indeed my routine every morning, but not without first drinking a glass of water.

"I have what you need, how much do you want?" I heard an almost imperceptible voice emanating from beneath the electric stove.

"Whaaat?!" I immediately responded while struggling in my mind to reject the idea of talking cockroaches. I couldn't believe it; I was hearing Chilo's voice again in his cockroach version, as in the... dream. "No, it's not true," I repeated to myself... and also aloud. "There's no cockroach under the stove," I emphasized my statement even more. "Much less looking like that dear friend."

Then, I moved the stove from its place, and a cockroach scurried away, displaying on its face a grimace of annoyance, almost bordering on disdain or hatred, which, without uttering a word, turned around to disappear as it turned a nearby corner.

THE END

Based on
Real-Life Events

www.ingramcontent.com/pod-product-compliance
Lightning Source LLC
LaVergne TN
LVHW041541060526
838200LV00037B/1087